Reneé Conde

Get the message?

"Look what you did!" Virginia yelled, fiddling with her broken glasses.

"You can put them together with a safety pin," Darlene said. "They're not really broken."

"They're the only pair I've got for the competition," said Virginia. "I'll look great in front of the judges." She glared at Darlene. "I think you did it on purpose! You're just nasty. All you people are nasty."

"We are not!" Cindi protested.

"I wasn't talking about you," said Virginia. She stared at Darlene.

"I think I know what she meant," Darlene said softly.

**Look for these and other books
in THE GYMNASTS series:**

THE GYMNASTS

#15 NASTY COMPETITION

Elizabeth Levy

AN
APPLE
PAPERBACK

SCHOLASTIC INC.
New York Toronto London Auckland Sydney

ISBN 0-590-43833-6

Copyright © 1991 by Elizabeth Levy.
All rights reserved. Published by Scholastic Inc.
APPLE PAPERBACKS is a registered trademark of Scholastic Inc.
THE GYMNASTS is a trademark of Scholastic Inc.

12 11 10 9 8 7 6 5 4 3 2 1   1 2 3 4 5 6/9

Printed in the U.S.A.   40

First Scholastic printing, January 1991

To Nan — 25 years, and it's never been nasty.
Love, Liz

Cindi,
the Closet Klutz

"If I hear that music one more time I'm going to barf," I said. I put my hands over my ears. Patrick was playing a tape of classical music he had gotten from the United States Gymnastics Federation. A woman's voice on the USGF tape told us what to do. I hated her voice. It was so prissy.

Call me Cindi, the closet klutz. I can do an eagle from the uneven bars. I can do a roundoff back flip leading into a back somersault on the floor. I just have no sense of rhythm. Even when Patrick shouts out "One, two, three, four," in time to the music, I can't hear the beat.

Patrick pulled my hands away from my ears. "Hands on the ears is not the correct position," he said as he turned off the cassette player.

I didn't trust myself to tell him what I thought the correct position might be.

"Could we just get back to doing something fun?" I grumbled.

"Cindi's idea of fun is a cartwheel on the beam," teased Darlene.

"Yes," I agreed, "even a layout vault. Gymnastics is supposed to be fast and tough, not prissy."

"It's not my fault the judges are concentrating more on dance," said Patrick. I had a feeling Patrick agreed with me that there was too much dance in gymnastics. "Look, Cindi, we have to work on the dance requirement. You girls are strong everywhere but dance. We're working on a whole new level here. Remember, we have to get ready for the state championships."

Nobody expected my team, the Pinecones, to reach the state championships. We had an incredible meet season this year. There was no denying we had improved far beyond what anybody expected.

"Cindi," said Patrick, "when you get to the state championships at Glenwood Springs, you can bet that the other teams will have their dance requirements down pat, and where will you kids be?"

"In the hot springs, I hope," I said.

I was excited about going to the state cham-

2

pionships in Glenwood Springs. It's supposed to have the world's largest warm swimming pool, because it's built right on natural hot springs. I've never been there, but I've heard about the hot pool.

I looked across the gym. Heidi Ferguson was doing her dance exercises at the bar. Every move looked perfect. Heidi has her own personal dance teacher. Heidi Ferguson is definitely not a Pinecone. We're an intermediate team, training in Denver, Colorado, at Patrick Harmon's Evergreen Gymnastics Academy.

Until Heidi came along, nobody paid much attention to us. Heidi is not just an elite gymnast, she's superelite. She was on the United States world championship team last year, and then she crashed — mentally, not physically. She got sick and stopped eating, and she was even going to quit gymnastics. Then she met us or, more important, my best friend, Lauren Baca. The next thing I knew, Heidi Ferguson had decided that the Evergreen Gymnastics Academy gym was going to be her personal training ground.

Heidi doesn't go to regular school. She takes correspondence courses for her academic work, and she sees her shrink. Then she gets private lessons from Patrick and private lessons from her dance coach. I think Heidi probably has a private coach for brushing her teeth. Her parents are sports nuts. Their son, Chris, is a great free-style skier, and he works out in our gym, too. He's away for a month training in Lake Placid, New York.

Heidi and Chris's mother is a piece of work. She seems to leave Chris alone, maybe because nobody expects Chris to win a gold medal. Heidi's mom's whole life is wrapped up in Heidi's career.

There is nothing regular about Heidi, and there's been nothing regular about the Pinecones since Heidi started hanging out with us.

Heidi took a break and came over to watch us work out our dance routine.

"Fifth position, fifth position!" Patrick shouted. "You've got to start the *pas ballotté* in fifth. Move your arms, Cindi. Your arms are not supposed to hang there like limp spaghetti."

"I'd like to put a finger up the nose of the idiot who decided that a gymnast has to dance," I whispered. Lauren giggled. She didn't like dance any more than I did, but at least she is better at it than I am.

"Heidi?" asked Patrick. "Would you mind doing the combination across the floor and letting the Pinecones follow you?"

"I'd love to," said Heidi.

"I don't see why Heidi spends so much time with the Pinecones," muttered Becky Dyson as the advanced girls waited for their rotation on

4

the dance mats. Becky is an advanced gymnast, but she's nowhere as good as Heidi. I think it galls her that Heidi has declared herself an honorary Pinecone.

It is weird. Heidi thinks we bring her good luck or something. She's making a comeback. We'll see how she does at the state championships. She should easily win the all-around. Becky would love it if Heidi loses. It would prove that the Pinecones are bad luck.

Of course, *we* could get wiped out at the state championships. None of the Pinecones seemed to care about how *we* were going to do. All we worried about was Heidi's mental health.

Personally I thought my own mental health was going downhill just because of the stupid dance requirements.

One by one the Pinecones moved across the floor. Darlene was the best. She's tall and graceful. Her mom's a model, and her dad's a football player. Even though "Big Beef" Broderick weighs around two hundred and fifty pounds, he can move as quickly as a cougar pouncing on a rabbit.

Ti An moved across the floor after Darlene. Ti An is tiny and light on her feet. She's Vietnamese American, and every move she makes is elegant.

Ashley Frank was next. Ashley is only nine. She's Ti An's age, but she's not as cute as Ti An.

Of course, Ashley doesn't think that. Ashley thinks that, with her little brown pigtails, she's the cutest thing on earth.

Ashley's not as graceful as Ti An, but she made it across with no mistakes and without tripping.

My dad is an airline pilot. He's got quick reflexes, which I've inherited. Unfortunately Dad also has two left feet. Mom says that even in the sixties when everybody was supposed to do "their own thing," Dad's dancing was so awkward and gawky that it was pathetic. I'm afraid I've inherited his dancing genes.

"Let's go, Cindi," said Patrick. "It's your turn. Everybody's doing beautifully."

"It's not fair," I complained. "My dad was born with two left feet. My ancestors tripped on the gangplank off the boat from England."

"No excuses," said Patrick, but at least I had made him laugh. That was something.

Unfortunately as I tried to dance across the floor, I knew I would make the judges laugh, too. That wasn't something to wish for.

Airy Armpits

A week later we were working on our dance routine when Heidi's dance teacher entered the gym. She was a tall woman, who looked to be in about her sixties, except that her hair was jet-black. She walked with a slight limp and carried a wooden cane with a burnished silver top. She wore her hair up in an elaborate French twist, and she almost never smiled. Her name was Madame Maria, and I found her scary.

She came over and stood next to Patrick, leaning on her cane. "What are they doing?" she asked.

"We're practicing the level six dance routine. It's what they'll have to do for the state championships," Patrick replied.

Madame Maria took out a pair of half glasses and peered down at Patrick's book. Then she looked up at us. "The secret to the success of the cabriole is in the arms," she said.

"It sounds like an Italian dish that would be good to eat," said Lauren.

"I think it sounds more like a wild animal that lives up in the mountains," I joked. "The cabriole that ate downtown Denver."

"Is that supposed to be funny?" asked Madame Maria, peering at me over the top of her glasses.

I shuffled my feet uneasily. I wished she would go away and work with Heidi. She was making me nervous.

Patrick clapped his hands.

"Girls," said Patrick. "You all have seen Madame Maria working with Heidi. She was once a leading dancer in the Soviet Union, and now she is a renowned teacher. I have a great treat for you. Madame Maria knows that we are trying to fine-tune our performance for the state championships. She has very graciously accepted Heidi's invitation to give the Pinecones some pointers."

"Patrick," I whined. "Nothing personal, Madame Maria, but aren't we ever going to get back to gymnastics?"

Madame Maria frowned at me. "What is your

name, young lady, you with the outlandish red hair."

I flipped my long red hair back. My hair is thick and curly, so it always looks a little messy, but I *like* my hair.

"Cindi Jockett," I muttered.

"Well, Cindi Jockett," said Madame Maria. She had a Russian accent, and she made Jockett sound weird. "With that attitude, you will not get far, young lady."

Ashley raised her hand. "Madame Maria," chirped Ashley, "I think it's wonderful that you're going to help us."

"Teacher's pet," I muttered.

"A real dance teacher could make all the difference," said Ashley.

"At least give Madame Maria a chance," whispered Darlene.

Patrick went to work with Heidi and left us alone with Madame Maria. She rapped her cane on the mat. It made a soft thudding noise.

"Young la*dies*," she said, emphasizing the wrong syllable. "Ballet is a matter of attitude as well as skill. In ballet as well as gymnastics, you are asking the audience to *look* at you . . . to pay attention. You must reward them." She rolled the word *reward* around her tongue.

I sighed and shifted my weight from one foot

to the other. The only reward I was interested in was getting back to gymnastics. Across the gym, Heidi was doing giant circles around the high bar with Patrick spotting her. That's what I wanted to be doing, not listening to Madame Maria chirp at me.

"You there," said Madame Maria. She pointed her cane at Darlene. Darlene stepped forward. She curtsied. Jodi and I giggled.

Madame Maria lifted her chin. "Who is imitating the hyena?" she asked.

I shut my mouth and lifted my own chin. I didn't like being called a hyena.

"All right," said Madame Maria. "Now, would the negress please try going across the floor, doing cabrioles." Madame Maria pointed her cane at Darlene.

"Excuse me?" asked Darlene. I couldn't believe my ears, myself.

"You," said Madame Maria. "You do know what a cabriole is. You start in *demi-plié*, swing your left foot forward, and beat your calves together landing on the right leg. Then repeat."

"I know what a cabriole is," said Darlene. "But I don't think you know my name. It's Darlene. Not Negress."

I was proud of Darlene for standing up to her. Madame Maria stamped her cane "I'm sorry. My

10

English is not so good. Now, please, let me see you move across the floor."

Darlene took a deep breath. She moved across the floor, keeping her rib cage lifted. Every time she jumped beating her legs together, she went a little higher. Each jump was better than the one before. She was the best dancer of any of us.

Madame Maria frowned. She didn't even praise her. "Next!" she said. "You, there, the blonde who was giggling."

Jodi stepped forward. "I'm not very good at dance," she said. Jodi wasn't being modest. She was telling the truth. Jodi and I were the worst dancers on the team. Well, maybe Lauren wasn't very good, either.

Jodi tried the cabriole. When Darlene did it, she made it look like a natural way to almost fly across the mats. Jodi looked as if her two legs were glued together.

To my surprise, Madame Maria smiled. "Yes, there is potential."

Jodi rolled her eyes. She is always hearing about her potential.

Madame Maria looked over the rest of us standing in line. Ti An, Ashley, Lauren, and me.

"All right," she said. "It is now the turn of the gorgeous redhead."

My head jerked forward. "Gorgeous? Me?"

"Step forward, *ma petite*!" Now I knew she was nuts. Not only am I not gorgeous, but I'm certainly not petite. I've grown three inches this year alone. I don't like it. Being tall is not an advantage in gymnastics. I'm nearly as tall as Darlene, and she's two years older than I am.

I stood where I was. Madame Maria pointed her dreaded cane at me. "I was speaking to you, Cindi," she said. "I want you to do the cabriole."

"I can't do it half as well as Darlene," I muttered.

"I will be the judge of that," said Madame Maria.

"Go for it, gorgeous," teased Lauren.

"You there," said Madame Maria. "This is a class . . . not a time for gossip. Please keep your comments to yourself."

"At least she didn't call you a hyena," I muttered. Madame Maria was giving me a pain in the neck.

"Now, Cindi," said Madame Maria. "As you do the cabriole, you must think of yourself as a princess . . . you have the world at your feet, and you jump for the sheer joy of it. Think airy armpits. Airy armpits."

I laughed so hard I was snorting. I couldn't help myself. Lauren started giggling.

Madame Maria pounded her cane on the mat.

12

"Cindi," she frowned. "I did not make a joke."

"Yes, Madame Maria," I said, but I couldn't stop giggling.

I took a deep breath and started across the mats, but on my very first jump my ankles crossed, I came down on the wrong foot and got my right foot tangled up with my left foot. I couldn't go anywhere.

"Whoops," I said, still giggling. "I think I tripped on the world."

"Never mind," said Madame Maria. "You have a very good body for ballet. We just have to work on the fine points. Now do it again."

I managed to get across the floor without tripping. "Very good, very good, Cindi . . . but remember to point the toes, dear."

I stood next to Darlene. "Airy armpits," I gasped out.

Darlene was watching as Ti An floated across the floor, doing the cabriole ever so gracefully.

"I can't believe what she called you," I said to Darlene. "I think we should tell Patrick."

"Oh, Cindi," said Darlene. "Don't get worked up about it. It's probably just how she learned English."

"You don't think she's prejudiced?" I asked.

Darlene shook her head. "I love ballet," she said. "We can learn so much from her. It will really help us. Let's give her the benefit of the doubt."

"I don't like her," I said.

"You're just embarrassed because she called you gorgeous," teased Darlene.

3

Don't Look a Gift Horse in the Mouth

I was beginning to feel that a day without Madame Maria was like a day without school. Finally we were moving. We were working on the first pass of our floor routine, a roundoff flic-flac to a tucked back salto. I even liked the sound of the words, nothing French. The terms might sound strange to somebody who doesn't take gymnastics. It's just a cartwheel with a half-turn, a back handspring, and a back somersault flying through the air. Now, that's my idea of fun! It's the hardest tumbling run I've ever done in my life. I was hoping to wow the judges with it at the state championships.

Patrick stood in the middle of the floor mats,

spotting us. I still needed a little help getting the back salto.

I took off. I love my tumbling passes on the floor routine. I don't really listen to the music. I just stand on the edge of the mat, and then I explode to the other corner. Everything else gets blocked out.

I leaped high into the air after my flic-flac. I knew I needed all the height I could get. I waited until the top to throw my knees over my head. Patrick just had to tap me on my back in order for me to make it around. I finished a little off balance, but it was the best pass I had made in a week.

"Great, Cindi," said Patrick. "Just concentrate on the landing. Lunge on the right leg, *demi-plié*, stretching your left leg backward."

"Don't say that word, '*demi-plié*,' " I begged him.

Patrick shook his head. "Madame Maria tells me that she thinks you have great potential."

Jodi snorted. "Uh-oh, the dreaded *p* word."

I giggled. Jodi and I both hate it when teachers talk about our "potential." It only means they want to tell our parents to make us work harder.

I watched as Darlene did her tumbling pass. She had trouble getting enough height on the back somersault, and she ended up falling to her knees, even with Patrick's spotting.

16

Heidi came over and watched with us. She shook her head. "Darlene's got to get more punch," she said.

"Well, this is a hard pass for her," I said.

"You have only a couple of weeks before we go to Glenwood Springs," said Heidi.

"She'll get it," I said. "If she doesn't, it's not the end of the world."

"Yeah," said Jodi, "we've lost meets on the local level. We can lose on the state level."

"Who knows?" I teased. "If we put our minds to it, we could be world-class losers."

Heidi glared at me. "Cindi Jockett, you of all people shouldn't talk like that."

"Hey, lighten up, Heidi," I said. "I was just kidding. And why me of all people?"

"Because you have the potential to be a real winner," said Heidi.

"Uh-oh," said Jodi. "There's the *p* word again, Cindi."

I didn't like Heidi singling me out as if I were different from the other Pinecones. As far as I was concerned it was all or nothing with the Pinecones. The one thing I liked about our team was that we stuck together, win *or* lose.

"Forget about potential," I said to Heidi.

"You're right," snapped Heidi, not under-standing what I meant. "Potential is nothing. You have to do something with it."

Lauren was doing her tumbling pass. She didn't get enough height, either, and couldn't make it around without a heavy spot from Patrick. I could hear Heidi mutter under her breath.

"What's wrong?" I asked.

"Nothing," said Heidi. "I just wanted Lauren to try harder."

"She *is* trying harder," I said. "I suppose you think that Lauren's a drag on the team, too," I said.

"I didn't say that," objected Heidi.

Darlene came up to us, still out of breath from her tumbling pass. "This tumbling pass is a joke," said Darlene. "I'll never get it."

"At least you'll do terrifically on the dance part," I said. "I get the tumbling and then I lose just as many points doing the stupid arabesque balance."

"You've got to think of the floor routine as a combination," said Heidi. "The dance and the tumbling should come together."

"Easy for you to say," I noted. "Everything comes together for you."

"Not that easily," said Heidi. "I work at it."

"I know that," I admitted.

"All you have to do is listen to what Madame Maria says," urged Heidi. "I know she likes you, Cindi. Seriously, she says you have the perfect dancer's body. But she complains that you're not working hard enough."

"Darlene is a much better dancer than I am," I objected. "I don't think Madame Maria knows anything. I don't know why she likes me."

"Don't look a gift horse in the mouth," said Darlene.

I shrugged. Madame Maria was a gift horse from Heidi. Sometimes I wasn't sure that I wanted either one — Madame Maria or Heidi.

4

Don't Rock the Boat

"*Plié*, arabesque, balance, forward *passé*." Madame Maria's commands rang out across the gym. We had only one week before we left for the state championships, and Madame Maria was now working with us three times a week. Suddenly I was looking forward to the state championships just to get away from that Russian accent.

Madame Maria clapped her hands together. "Darlene, what are you doing?" she demanded.

Darlene had been balanced on her right leg, her left leg stretched backward and upward, her body leaning forward. Her left leg was pointed beautifully. Even her armpits were airy.

Darlene wobbled and started to bring her leg down.

"I did not tell you to release the pose," said Madame Maria. "Your leg — it is flopping there like the tail of a monkey. You are not supposed to be a monkey, you are supposed to be a dancer."

I could see Darlene biting her lip from the effort to keep balanced on one foot. Madame Maria took her cane and tapped Darlene's leg.

"Higher . . . higher . . ." she insisted. Finally Darlene lost her balance completely.

Darlene rolled her eyes. She had really held the pose longer than was humanly possible.

"Sorry, Madame Maria," said Darlene.

"The judges are not going to want to look at a monkey. They want to see dancers."

"What!?" I exploded. I had had enough. It seemed to me that Madame Maria had no right to call Darlene a monkey.

Madame Maria turned to me. "Excuse me, Cindi?" she asked.

I looked over at Darlene feeling totally confused. Darlene can be quiet, but Darlene isn't a mouse. She's the oldest Pinecone. She's even captain of the team. Darlene isn't one to let *anybody* insult her, even a Russian prima donna.

Darlene shook her head at me. "It's okay, Cindi," she said.

"Cindi?" asked Madame Maria in that voice I hated.

"I . . . uh . . ." I couldn't just say nothing. "I think that Darlene is one of the best dancers of the Pinecones. I don't understand what you mean, calling her a monkey."

Madame Maria's dark eyes narrowed at me. "Cindi, my dear, everything I say is with a purpose. I want Darlene to improve. I want *you* to improve. With your long legs and short torso, you have the perfect body for ballet. Life is simply not fair sometimes."

I've noticed that whenever adults start spouting that line about "Life isn't fair," they're usually covering up something.

I looked over at Darlene. I knew her as well as anybody. Darlene is long-legged and short-waisted, too. As far as I can tell, the only real difference between us is that Darlene is black, and I am white.

"Now," continued Madame Maria, "Cindi, I suggest you stop worrying about Darlene and worry about yourself. Let me see you do the combination across the floor."

I gritted my teeth. I was so mad I couldn't hold the arabesque. My leg wobbled all over the place.

Madame Maria stood behind me and held my leg for me in the correct position. "Good, Cindi . . . very good."

I glanced at Darlene, but she just looked away. Finally the dance class was over. We did some cool-downs and headed for the locker room.

My brother Jared stopped me. Jared works out with the boys' team.

"Hey, Cindi, you look really steamed," he said. I've got to admit that he knows me better than anybody else.

"It's the new dance teacher," I said. "I *hate* her."

Jared raised one eyebrow. He's always been able to do that. "Whoa!" he said. "What did she do to you?"

"She likes me," I exploded. "That's the problem!"

"Oh," said Jared, "that explains it."

"You don't understand," I pleaded with him. "I think she's a racist. She picks on Darlene."

"Are you sure?" Jared asked. "That's a pretty serious accusation. Does Darlene agree with you?"

"I don't know," I admitted. "But I'm sure I'm right."

"Maybe you should check with Darlene," suggested Jared. "She's the one who should be complaining, not you."

"I know, I know . . . but Madame Maria's so creepy."

"I wouldn't rock the boat one week before the competition," said Jared.

"Jared, are you telling me to do nothing?" I yelled at him.

Jared backed off. "No, but at least find out what Darlene thinks before you go off half-cocked."

"I am not going off half-cocked," I said.

Jared raised one eyebrow.

"All right . . . all right," I said. "I'll find out exactly what Darlene thinks, and then . . . we'll nail Madame Maria's hide to the wall."

"That certainly sounds like a calm, measured approach," said Jared.

5

Competition Nastier Than the Atomic Amazons

I left Jared and pushed through the swinging door into the locker room. "The old witch!" I exploded as soon as the locker room door closed behind me.

"What are you complaining about now?" demanded Becky. I hadn't even realized she was in the locker room. So was Heidi. Heidi looked at me expectantly.

"Your Madame Maria is some piece of work," I said to Heidi.

"First of all, she's not *my* Madame Maria," said Heidi.

"Cindi, cool it," said Darlene softly. "You're overreacting."

"You're underreacting," I said. "How could you take what she said to you?"

"What did Madame Maria say to Darlene?" Heidi asked.

"She called her a monkey. She treats Darlene as if she's just come from the jungle. I *know* the only reason she picks on her is because Darlene's black."

"Whoa!" said Heidi. "I think that's a mighty big jump. Madame Maria is just very expressive. She uses expressive language."

"Yeah? Well, I think her expressive language is against the law."

"Do you think Madame Maria is racist?" Heidi asked Darlene.

Darlene sighed. "I don't know. I sure can't do anything right for her. Still, she tries to help me. I just couldn't hold the arabesque long enough to suit her."

"I held it for a mini-second, and I get 'Very good, Cindi.' "

"That doesn't make her racist," said Heidi. "Face it, Cindi. You didn't go into dance classes without any prejudices of your own. To be the best gymnast, you have to take dance seriously. You think you can slide around it. You were prejudiced against Madame Maria from the beginning."

"She's got a point," said Lauren.

"Maybe," I admitted. "But that doesn't make what Madame Maria's doing right."

"Look," said Darlene, "I don't like Madame Maria calling me a monkey, but if it means I pick up a couple of extra tenths of a point at the state competitions, I'm willing to take it."

"Your father wouldn't take it," I said to Darlene.

"You don't know that," she retorted. "You can't know what it's like to be black. Dad told me he took all kinds of abuse from some of his white coaches, but he still learned from them. He says that you have to learn from everybody."

I shook my head. "I don't believe you," I said. "I mean, it's so clear to me that Madame Maria likes Jodi and me just because we're the right color."

"Thanks a bunch," said Jodi. "I thought finally I had found a teacher who didn't immediately think I was hopeless."

"Be honest," I said. "Jodi, you know that Darlene can dance circles around both of us."

"Hey, does anybody here remember that you have a state championship to get ready for in just a week?" said Heidi. "You Pinecones shouldn't be wasting your time and energy worrying about this stuff. You've got more important things to worry about."

"Heidi's right," said Lauren.

I put my hands on my hips. It seemed to me lately that all Lauren could say was "Heidi's right."

"I liked it better when you used to say 'It's a proven fact.' Now the only proof you need is Heidi's word."

"Hey, Cindi," said Lauren. "You're out of line. What did I do?"

I blinked. I was lashing out at my teammates at the worst possible moment. Maybe I was the one in the wrong. I took a deep breath. "Sorry," I mumbled.

"Cindi," said Heidi, "I've been around a lot of major competitions. I've seen teams get uptight like this. You're looking for a scapegoat for all your tensions, and Madame Maria is it. She's not an ogre."

"Are you going to snap off my head if I say 'Heidi's right'?" asked Lauren.

I shook my head. "No," I said. "I guess I'm the one who should be sorry."

"Forget it," said Darlene. "I like the fact that you wanted to stand up for me, even if it wasn't totally necessary."

Heidi looked relieved. She smiled. "Come on, guys," she said. "The reason I like the Pinecones is that you're so loosey-goosey. Lighten up, Cindi."

Darlene and I glanced at each other.

"You really think I was overreacting?" I said.

"Well, if I ever need a champion, I know I can count on you," said Darlene. "Let me fight my own battles, okay? Madame Maria isn't our problem. Think of all the teams we've got to face at the state championships."

I screwed up my face.

"You know," said Lauren, "it's just like you to get uptight right before a big competition."

"Thanks a bunch," I said.

"Cindi?" asked Jodi. "Cindi's always cool under pressure."

"During the event," said Lauren. "But before she's a bundle of nerves."

I didn't like my team analyzing me. It made me feel uncomfortable, even if they were right.

"I don't blame you for being nervous," said Heidi. "You guys thought the Atomic Amazons were tough. Wait till you meet some of the teams from small towns. They've got gymnasts out in the boondocks who do nothing but eat, sleep, and dream gymnastics. Some of my toughest competition always come from towns you've never even heard of."

"Oh, great," I sighed. "That's just what we need, competition nastier than the Atomic Amazons."

6

The Old Witch
Can Dance

"She's what?" I exclaimed to Patrick.

"Madame Maria has agreed to be a chaperon for the state championships. She feels that she'll be able to give you guidance up to the last moment. And she wants to be there for Heidi, too."

"Talk about the kiss of death," I whispered to Lauren.

Patrick heard me. "Cindi," he asked in a warning tone, "what *is* the problem?"

I didn't know exactly how to answer him.

"Cindi?" repeated Patrick.

Patrick isn't one of those adults who asks you questions and then doesn't listen. If something's bothering you, Patrick wants to know.

30

I sighed. "I can't explain it," I said. "Madame Maria is just . . . "

"Oh, Cindi," said Darlene, sounding exasperated.

I looked at her. If Darlene wasn't upset about Madame Maria, I guess it wasn't my place to call her a racist in front of Patrick.

I looked around at my fellow Pinecones, hoping for a little support, but after our locker room conversation the other day, I knew they thought I was out of line about Madame Maria.

"Nothing," I said softly.

"I've been pleased with the changes I've seen in the Pinecones since you've been working with Madame Maria," said Patrick. "Particularly in *your* floor routine, Cindi."

"Thanks," I said.

Patrick gazed at me a beat longer than necessary. I guess he could tell I was being a little sarcastic.

"I mean it," he said.

"I did say thank you," I insisted.

"And I know Madame Maria is very happy with the work the Pinecones have been doing. She has told me that she sees improvement in all of you. It's been a great relief for me to get somebody to teach you dance who knows what she's doing. She is coming in today, even though she's not scheduled, just to watch our floor routines and to add some final flourishes. I trust her taste absolutely. This is exactly what we have needed."

"Don't you think you're taking this too far?" I asked Patrick. "We did all right before we had Madame Maria."

Patrick shook his head. "Cindi, gymnastics is the blend of dance skills and athletics."

"That's the way Heidi talks," I said.

"And who would know better?" asked Patrick. "Here comes Madame Maria now."

Madame Maria walked into the gym. She smiled at Patrick. "Good afternoon," she said, flinging off her cape and handing it to Patrick as if he were some guy in a restaurant.

I wanted Patrick to plop it back on her head, but he very meekly took it and hung it on a coat-rack in the corner of the gym.

My brother and the boys' group stopped to stare. I didn't blame them. Madame Maria was wearing a black leotard with a bright-pink satin wraparound miniskirt. It looked ridiculous on somebody her age. And she was supposed to give us pointers on good taste.

"All right," said Patrick. "Ashley, why don't you go first?"

Ashley did her routine. She started with a body wave. Even I could see that her arm gestures were more fluid than they were before Madame Maria had started to work with us, but she came down heavily from her tumbling.

"Very fine!" said Madame Maria. "But you must always think, 'Raise my chin, raise my chin.' The judges want to see your beautiful eyes."

Ashley beamed. Ashley loves flattery.

"Okay, Ti An," said Patrick.

Ti An's shoulders went up and down from nervousness. She twisted her head back and forth to get the kinks out. Then she stood on the correct position on the mats and did her body waves. With Ti An, I really could see that Madame Maria had taught her something. Every element of her routine flowed into the next.

"Beautiful, Ti An," said Madame Maria. "You will make the judges believe that you float like a butterfly. . . ."

Ti An nodded.

"A butterfly with airy armpits," I guffawed.

Ti An giggled.

Madame Maria turned to me. "Cindi, you must not always make the jokes. Let me see you do your routine without the jokes."

I went out onto the mats and crossed my arms over my chest, the position with which I started my routine. Patrick punched the music on the cassette player. Madame Maria watched me, tapping out the beat of the music with her cane.

"The chin . . . the chin," she shouted out to me. "You must let the judges see your eyes. They want to see your beautiful face. You must make the judges feel that you *love* the music."

I stopped. "I don't *looove* the music," I said, imitating Madame Maria's accent. I knew I was being rude, but I couldn't help myself.

"Cindi," said Madame Maria, coming out on the mats, and soothing her skirt. "The judges do not care what you *really* think. I do not care what you *think*. I care how you dance. You must convince the judges and me that you are a dancer."

"But I'm *not* a dancer," I protested.

"That is only in your mind," said Madame Maria. "I am an old lady. I have a limp from an old dance injury, but I can make you believe I am still a dancer."

Madame Maria took my pose, crossing her arms in front of her chest. In one way, she looked incredibly silly, a sixty-year-old lady, her chin high in the air. Yet, I couldn't keep my eyes off her. Her arms flowed from her torso, and although I might hate the old witch, I had to admit she could dance.

"All right," said Madame Maria. "Now, Cindi, you do it again, and this time, you fool me *and* the judges. You pretend you *are* a dancer."

7

Winning *Is* Fun

The state championships started very early on Saturday morning, and all of us had had to get permission to miss a day of school so that we could get to Glenwood Springs by Friday afternoon. Patrick wanted us to have time to rest.

This was only the second time in my life that I had gotten out of school for gymnastics. It was a five-hour train trip to Glenwood Springs. I couldn't imagine what we were going to do for five hours.

I'd never taken a train trip. I've been on airplanes all my life. We get to fly free because of Dad being a pilot. I've been to Hawaii and Disney

World. I've taken buses and every kind of car trip. With four older brothers you do get to ride in a lot of cars, but I had never taken a train.

"I love trains," said Dad as he took Lauren, Jodi, and me to the train station. "I wish I were coming with you. But I've got to work this weekend."

"I can't believe you love trains," said Jodi. "I would think they'd be too slow for you."

"No, trains are wonderful," said Dad. "You girls are in for a treat. The train trip to Glenwood Springs is one of the prettiest in the country."

"It takes so long," I said. "I mean, we could fly to Disney World in less time."

"There's no airport in Glenwood Springs," said Dad. "It's a small town."

"I brought lots of books to read," said Lauren, "and candy to eat." Lauren loves food.

"They sell food on the train," I said.

Dad pulled up in front of the train station at the same time that Darlene was getting her suitcase out of her father's trunk.

"Darlene, how much did you bring?" I asked. Darlene's dad was lugging a big garment bag over his shoulder. I had a small duffel bag in which I had rolled up my clean competition leotard and a practice leotard. I had a pair of jeans and my bicycle pants, my old shocking-pink windbreaker, and a bathing suit. I didn't think that I needed anything else.

"Yeah," said Lauren, "we're only going for a weekend."

"I didn't bring that much," said Darlene, defensively.

"Right," said her dad. "She didn't take the really big suitcase with the wheels."

"What did you bring besides your leotards?" I asked her.

Darlene grinned. "Well, I brought a couple of party dresses," she admitted. "I figured that there are going to be a lot of kids from all over the state. There are bound to be a few parties."

"I bet you wish Chris were coming," teased Heidi. Darlene and Heidi's brother are dating. "Too bad he's in Lake Placid."

"I didn't bring any dresses," I said. "I never thought about parties."

"Don't worry," said Big Beef. "I'm sure Darlene brought more than enough for all the Pinecones."

"Yeah," joked Lauren. "I'd look great in one of Darlene's dresses." Lauren's about half the size of Darlene. "Cindi's the only one who would fit into one, and Cindi never wears dresses."

"I travel light," I said.

"You did bring bathing suits for the hot tub, didn't you?" asked Darlene.

"*A* bathing suit," I said.

Patrick was standing in the middle of the train station with all of our tickets.

"Do you want to sit together?" Darlene asked me.

"Sure," I said, looking down at my jeans and long sleeved T-shirt. "Are you sure you're not ashamed to be seen with me?"

Darlene laughed. "No. Let's get our tickets from Patrick, before Madame Maria gets here."

"I thought you liked her," I said to Darlene.

"Not so much that I want to sit near her," said Darlene. Heidi and her mother came up to Patrick. Heidi's mom was fussing over her.

"I don't understand," she complained. "I feel it's wrong that I'm not going to be there. This is your first meet since, you know. . . ." Her voice lowered.

"Since I was hospitalized for anorexia," said Heidi in a loud voice.

Mrs. Ferguson looked around. "Heidi," she hissed, "this is a public place. You never know what competitors might be around."

Heidi's mother had the same jet-black hair as Madame Maria. Maybe that's why I had taken an instant dislike to Madame Maria.

Heidi saw me standing there and winked at me. "Hi, Cindi!"

"Hi, Heidi." I grinned. "Hi, Heidi" sounds silly. Heidi was carrying a knapsack.

"That's all you're carrying?" I asked.

Heidi's eyes traveled down to a huge duffel bag at her feet. "I've got about a dozen different pairs of gymnastics shoes that I need to take to every tournament."

"What for?" I asked.

"I never know which ones are going to *feel* right," said Heidi. "I've got my lucky ones from the world championships, but they're worn out. I've got my ones from the McDonald's Cup. It's a tradition. I always bring along whatever shoes won me a championship."

Heidi's mother was tapping her foot impatiently. "Heidi," she snapped, "I'm sure Cindi will have plenty of time to *see* your gymnastic shoes in Glenwood Springs, but this is *my* last time to talk to you."

"Mom," whined Heidi. It was strange to hear a world champion whining. I felt sorry for Heidi, and a little proud of her. It hadn't been easy telling her mother that she wanted to go to the state championships just with the Pinecones, and not with the whole family entourage.

"I've been over this again and again with you,"

said Heidi. "If I'm going to go on in gymnastics, I've got to do it my way."

"I'll see you on the train," I said to Heidi. I had a feeling that I was getting in the middle of a family discussion where I didn't belong.

Just then Madame Maria came bustling into the train station wearing her cape with a ridiculous multicolored scarf flowing behind her.

"I was so worried I would be late," she said. She grabbed my shoulder.

"I've got your ticket, Madame Maria," said Patrick.

"Good!" said Madame Maria. "Then we can all go together."

"So that's your Madame Maria," my father whispered to me as he gave me a good-bye kiss.

"She's not *my* Madame Maria," I said. Madame Maria turned to Dad.

"You must be Cindi's father," she said. "You have the same coloring."

"There's no denying that," said Dad, rubbing his hand through his red hair. "Unfortunately Cindi claims that she also inherited my two left feet in dancing."

"Oh, no," said Madame Maria, shaking Dad's hand enthusiastically. "Cindi has a lot of hidden talent."

"Come on, girls," said Patrick. "I want to get everybody settled on the train."

40

I gave my dad a last hug. "Good luck," he said. "And remember, have fun."

"Aren't you going to tell me to win?" I teased him.

Dad shook his head. "Naw, just have fun, but remember, winning *is* a lot of fun."

8

Heidi's a Strange Bird

The conductor stood on the platform and actually boomed out: "All a-bo-aard!"

I giggled. "It's just like a movie," I said to Darlene.

"Come on, girls, hustle," said Patrick. The train was a lot more crowded than I had expected.

We had to go through several cars before we could find a block of seats together. "I think I like airplanes a lot better."

"Give it a chance," said Darlene. Patrick gave Madame Maria a window seat. I felt a little sorry for Patrick, having to sit next to Madame Maria.

The train took off, only I guess that's the wrong

word. It gave a little jerk, and then we were moving out of the station.

I took a seat next to Darlene. The conductor helped Darlene get her garment bag on the rack over our heads. It stuck out and I was worried that when we went around a curve it would tumble down on top of us.

I looked out the window. All I could see were concrete walls on either side of the train. "So much for beautiful scenery," I said. "I like clouds. I like that feeling when it's a rainy day and you go up in an airplane and suddenly it's blue skies." I fumbled around in the cracks of my seat.

"What are you doing?" asked Darlene.

I started to laugh. "I was looking for my seat belt," I confessed.

Darlene shook her head. "And to think I wanted to sit next to you. I should have let you sit with Heidi."

"No, thanks," I said. "Heidi would probably talk my ear off about how independent she feels going to a meet without her mother."

"She says her shrink thinks it's a good idea."

"Shrink thinks," I repeated. "It would be weird to have a shrink, don't you think? Shrink is such a funny word."

"Don't make fun of it," said Darlene. "I think Heidi's got guts."

"Well, naturally," I said. "When you think of

the tricks she can do. I mean, she could break her neck. She does some release moves off the high bar that are killers."

"That's not what I'm talking about," said Darlene. "I think she's got guts to tell us she's going to a shrink. I think the pressure from her mom just got to be too much for her. I guess that's why she stopped eating. It can't be easy on her."

"Did you hear her arguing with her mom in the train station?" I asked.

"Arguing with your mom is better than starving yourself to get back at her," said Darlene. "I think it took courage for Heidi to tell her parents that she was going to this state championship and didn't want them to be there."

"Our parents come to our meets most of the time," I said. "You wouldn't tell your dad not to watch you."

"Yeah, but our parents don't drive us totally crazy," said Darlene.

"Speak for yourself," I said, but I had to admit Darlene was right.

I stood up and looked down the aisle of the train. Jodi and Lauren were sitting together, and right behind them were Ashley and Ti An. Heidi was sitting by herself, her legs stretched out along the extra seat. I felt a little guilty that Heidi had to sit by herself.

"I wonder if the Pinecones are really good for Heidi," I asked Darlene.

"I think so," said Darlene. "Without us she might have quit altogether."

"Do you think Heidi's good for us?" I asked.

"Absolutely," said Darlene. "She's already taught me a lot. We would never be going to these state championships if it weren't for her."

"I know," I admitted. "It's just that Heidi's so unpredictable. You never know what she's going to do next."

"Heidi's dramatic. That's why she's such a good performer. She *wants* the spotlight on her. It's the sign of a star," said Darlene.

"Now you're talking like Madame Maria."

"Madame Maria isn't always wrong," said Darlene.

"I still think she's prejudiced," I said.

"I don't," said Darlene. "I can tell. I don't *feel* she treats me any different because I'm black. She's just got old-fashioned ways of talking. I think she's a wonderful teacher."

The concrete walls on either side of the tracks became smaller and finally disappeared. We were moving through a section of warehouses outside Denver.

"Hey, guys! What are you two being so serious about?" asked Lauren.

"We were just talking," I said. Darlene had given me a lot to think about.

"Let's go up to the dining car," said Lauren.

"I thought you brought along enough candy to last a month," I teased.

"Yeah, but I want to see what else they've got," said Lauren.

"I'm hungry," said Ti An.

"Me, too," said Ashley.

We asked Patrick if he wanted us to bring back anything for him from the dining car. Madame Maria wanted black coffee. Naturally she'd ask for the one thing that would be the hardest to bring back.

"I think I'll stay here," said Heidi.

I grabbed her hand. "Come on," I insisted. Heidi smiled. Sometimes she seems so tough, and other times she seems shy, as if she needs protection. Heidi is a strange bird, but she's lucky in a way . . . lucky she has the Pinecones.

9

The Last Chance Team

There was a real dining car with white table-
cloths and a red rose on each table.

It felt as if we all should have been dressed in
one of Darlene's fancy dresses in order to eat
here. A maître d' in a red-and-gold Amtrak uni-
form came to our end of the dining car.

"How many are you?" he asked. "Are you here
for breakfast or for an early lunch?"

Darlene stepped forward. "Brunch," she said
as cool as could be. "And there are seven of us."

"I'm afraid I don't have a table for seven. You'll
have to split up. Come with me." He took the
first five, which left Heidi and me standing by
ourselves.

There were no more emply tables. "Brunch!" said Heidi. "I don't eat brunch."

Heidi has some mighty peculiar eating habits. She's better than she used to be. She eats regularly now, and she no longer starves herself, but she's still weird about food. She likes to eat the same thing every day. She has grapefruit juice and cornflakes for breakfast. A banana in the middle of the morning. A peanut-butter-and-banana sandwich for lunch. And boneless chicken for dinner.

When she first got out of the hospital, she had to keep a log of everything she ate so that her shrink would know she was really eating.

"Try a pancake for a change," I said. "It'll be good for you."

The maître d' came up to us. "I'm afraid I won't have a separate table for a long time, but I could put you with some other people, if you don't mind."

"Sure." I shrugged. We followed the maître d' to one of the tables where two girls about our age were sitting. One of them was a girl with short, very straight, light blonde hair with bangs that came down almost to her eyebrows. She wore thick glasses with heavy black frames that looked too big for her face. She was wearing a flower-print blouse. The girl sitting next to her had light brown hair that she wore back in a ponytail with a red ribbon around it that matched her red blouse.

Neither of them looked particularly happy we were going to be sitting next to them.

I introduced myself.

"I'm Heidi Katz," said Heidi quickly. I stared at her. Sometimes Heidi is paranoid about people recognizing her name. When she first got out of the hospital, her mother was worried about what the gymnastics press was going to say about it. Heidi's shrink convinced Heidi to just tell the truth about what happened to her.

I was very glad Heidi and her shrink had decided that the best thing would be to be honest. *If* Heidi goes to the Olympics, there's no way it wouldn't get out that she had been hospitalized for not eating. Somebody was bound to ask what a world-class athlete was doing hiding out with a group of intermediate kids. I couldn't figure out why she was back to lying.

"Did anybody ever tell you that you look just like the gymnast Heidi Ferguson?" asked the girl in the big glasses.

Heidi blushed.

"Are you girls gymnasts?" I asked quickly. I figured I'd try to give Heidi a chance to figure out what to say. It was stupid of Heidi to have lied again. I was sure that these kids were gymnasts, otherwise they would never have recognized her.

49

Heidi was famous, but only among kids who followed gymnastics. It wasn't as if she was on every box of cereal.

The girl with the big glasses nodded. "We're going to the state championships in Glenwood Springs. We're from Last Chance."

I laughed. "So are we. You guys shouldn't put yourself down like that."

Actually I was pleased that another team had even less confidence than the Pinecones. It made me feel a little bit superior, and it wasn't a feeling that I was used to as a Pinecone.

The girl with the glasses laughed so hard she started snorting. Lauren always tells me that I've got a laugh like that. She bobbed her head up and down, and a hooting noise came out of her.

Darlene and Lauren turned around in their seats and stared at us. I shrugged. I wasn't sure exactly what I had said that was so funny.

"We're *from* Last Chance," said the girl with the ponytail.

"Yeah, I heard you, but I still think you shouldn't keep saying that."

"The *town* of Last Chance," said the girl with the glasses. "In fact, last year we won the state championship in our category."

"What level do you compete in?" I asked with a sinking heart.

"Level six," said the girl with the ponytail. She

50

laughed at me. "How about you?"

"Level six," I admitted.

"And you thought we meant we didn't have a chance," she said, laughing at me. "Our town is on the plains, near Kansas. During the frontier days people called it Last Chance because once you got there, it was the last chance before you had to go over the Rockies and die."

"Now, all you have to do is go to Denver and die," said the girl with the glasses. "Denver is nothing but crime and pollution."

"I know," said the other girl. "I'm so glad that the championships are going to be held someplace where we don't have to breathe that air and worry about being mugged every second."

I wasn't sure how much I liked these kids putting down my hometown.

"I bet they're from Denver," said the girl with the glasses, pointing to Darlene's table.

"Those are my teammates," I said. "And Darlene's father is a Denver Bronco."

"The Broncos are a bunch of losers," said the girl with the big glasses. I hoped Darlene hadn't heard that.

"I wouldn't call them that," I said.

"What else would you call a football team that can't win the Super Bowl?" asked the girl with the ponytail.

"Winners," I said. "Think about the dozens of

teams that never even *get* to the Super Bowl."

The girl took off her glasses and twirled the earpiece in her hand.

"Still," said Heidi, "you've got to think something's wrong with a team when they can't win the big one."

The girl with the glasses nodded her head up and down. I couldn't take it. "Heidi Ferguson, you're all wet," I said.

The two girls stared at me. Then they turned back to Heidi. "Heidi Ferguson. You *are* Heidi Ferguson."

Heidi gave a silly grin. "Yeah," she said. "Thanks a bunch, Cindi."

"Yeah, Cindi," said the girl with the eyeglasses. "If Heidi Ferguson wanted to go incognito, you should have done what she wanted."

"Don't blame Cindi," said Heidi quickly. "I shouldn't have lied. I was just funning you."

"Funning you?" I asked. Heidi didn't usually talk like that.

"I figured that," said the girl with the glasses. She stuck her hand out. "Hi. My name is Virginia Peterson."

"And I'm Helen Johnson," said the girl with the ponytail. "Some people think I look like Brandy Johnson. That's why I thought maybe you were teasing about being Heidi Ferguson."

Heidi shook their hands warmly.

52

Virginia, the girl with the big glasses, leaned in toward the table "So," she said, "tell us the truth. Is Denver as bad as people say?"

"Absolutely not," I said.

The two girls looked as if they didn't believe me.

I looked out the window at the scenery.

10

She Sounded Human

The train had moved into the foothills of the Rockies, filled with low forests of scrub oak, just beginning to turn greenish yellow in the spring. The aspen trees hadn't begun to put out leaves yet.

Every now and then we passed a meager creek. Cottonwood and willow trees crowded one another at the waterside. The willow trees were bright green. I was beginning to understand why my dad liked trains. Some of the branches of the trees were so close to the tracks that it felt as if we were brushing by them as we moved. The scenery was beautiful, but it looked lonely to me without any houses or people.

Heidi and I finished our meal and said good-bye to the girls from Last Chance. Unfortunately we knew we'd meet again.

"I liked those girls," said Heidi. "They were real."

"Yeah, real weird," I said. "I *didn't* like them."

"Who?" asked Darlene, who was carrying the coffee back to Madame Maria. I had forgotten it, but Darlene hadn't. That's the kind of thoughtful person Darlene is.

"Those girls we were talking to in the dining car," I said. "They were from a town called Last Chance. Do you believe it?"

"They were sweet," said Heidi. "Stop being so prejudiced. Just because they were from a small town doesn't mean they were bad. You could have acted a little nicer to them. It always pays to be nice to the competition. It confuses them."

"More words of wisdom from Heidi Ferguson Katz," I teased.

"Heidi Ferguson Katz?" asked Ashley. "That's not your name."

"I know," giggled Heidi.

"Yeah, well, if you ask me, those kids from Last Chance should have stayed there."

"Why did you pretend to be somebody else?" Ashley asked.

"I knew right away those kids were gymnasts," said Heidi. "Cindi didn't. I just didn't want to have to answer any embarrassing questions."

"You just made things more embarrassing," I said.

"I went incognito for about sixty seconds, then Cindi here blew my cover," said Heidi.

"It was silly," I said. "You're competing under your own name at the state championships. Everybody at the meet is going to be looking for you."

"The blonde with the big black glasses? She's a gymnast?" asked Jodi. "She looked like a bookworm. She can't be so tough."

"They won last year," I said. "And they compete at level six."

"Now that I think about it," said Heidi. "I remember hearing about the team from Last Chance. They've got a very good coach. She's excellent."

"How come you know all this stuff and you were training out in California?" asked Jodi. "I never heard of the Last Chance team."

"That's because the Pinecones had their heads stuck in the sand before I got here," said Heidi. "You kids thought the Atomic Amazons were tough competition. You didn't realize how many hungry little gymnasts there are out there in the big world, and a lot of them are from small towns just like Last Chance. Mary Lou Retton was from a small town. Those are girls with a real hunger in their bellies."

"Oh, please," I said. "Give me a break."

"I've often got hunger in my belly," said Lauren. "And I'm from a big town."

"How could you be hungry after eating that big breakfast?" asked Heidi.

"Well, I have to admit that even my hunger is down a little after those pancakes," said Lauren.

"Heidi ate a whole third of her pancake," I said.

"Come on," said Heidi. "At least I ate some of it."

We kept jostling back and forth in the aisle as we made our way back. It was hard to walk and talk at the same time.

Patrick looked up from his seat. "I could hear the Pinecones a couple of cars away," he said. "You girls must have entertained the whole train with your conversation."

I blushed. We had been talking about some pretty embarrassing things. I had forgotten how many people could be listening. I hoped the Last Chance girls hadn't heard me bad-mouthing them.

Madame Maria looked up from the book she was reading. "When I traveled with my ballet troupe in the Soviet Union we once made so much noise dancing and singing that the conductor threw us off the train. We had to wait all day in the station for the next train, so we just continued laughing and singing and drinking."

I wondered if I had heard Madame Maria right. She sounded almost human. I had expected Madame Maria to yell at us for not acting properly on the train. Instead, she had a sly grin on her face. She reached out for the coffee.

"Thank you, Darlene dear," she said.

11

Do Pinecones Float?

Glenwood Springs stinks. Literally. The natural hot springs for which it is so famous are full of sulphur. It smells like rotten eggs.

We were staying in an old stone hotel right across the street from the hot springs. Teddy Roosevelt had stayed there when he was president about a hundred years ago. Back then it had been fashionable. Now, it just looked run-down.

Once, Glenwood Springs was as glamorous as Aspen. Back then people must have liked swimming in smelly pools much more than they liked skiing.

The hotel might have been fancy once, but it surely wasn't now. Late April is the time that everybody leaves Colorado, anyhow. It's called the "mud season." The snow is gone, but not much is green yet. All the gymnasts were staying at the old hotel. Darlene and I were staying in one room. Lauren and Jodi in another, and Ti An and Ashley in another. Heidi had her own room, naturally.

Lauren stuck her head in our room. "Put on your bathing suits," she said. "Let's go right to the pool."

"Is that okay with Patrick?" Darlene asked.

"Patrick's called a meeting for all the Pinecones down in the lobby in fifteen minutes," said Lauren. "I figure we should all show up in our bathing suits, and then he'll have to let us go."

Darlene held up two different bathing suits. One was a jungle print that looked like it was designed to save the rain forest. The other was bright orange.

"Which one should I wear?" she asked.

"The rain forest one," I said. "It's beautiful."

I had just brought my old turquoise suit from the summer before. The seat was practically worn out. I hoped it didn't dissolve in the sulphur.

"It's going to be so neat," said Lauren. "I'll go tell Heidi to put on her suit."

Patrick looked a little surprised when we all showed up in our bathing suits.

"You wanted us here so we could relax before the competition," said Lauren. "The hot springs are supposed to be very relaxing."

"Actually I think it's a good idea," said Patrick. "I just got a look at the official schedule. Since level six is the lowest level competing at the championships, we're first. They've scheduled you for eight-thirty A.M. That means you'll have to get up at six. I want you to eat a little toast, but you'll need time to digest."

Darlene groaned. She was definitely not a morning person.

"I think the most important thing is for you to relax before then," said Patrick. "So go to the hot springs and have a good time. I want you to get the kinks out from the long train ride."

"It's a proven fact that the waters from the hot springs are good for you," said Lauren. "The Indians thought that the hot springs were a sacred place. The water from the vapor caves is supposed to cure arthritis and asthma."

"How do you know all this stuff, already?" asked Darlene. "We just got here."

"I read the brochure in my room," said Lauren. "It was the first thing I did."

"The first thing I did was unpack," said Darlene.

Patrick sighed. "Girls, it's cool out there. Don't

stay too long at the hot springs. I don't want you catching colds."

"Patrick!" said Lauren. "The hot springs' natural temperature is nearly a hundred and thirty degrees. They have to cool it down to keep the little pool at a hundred and ten degrees. The big Olympic swimming pool is kept at eighty-five. Teddy Roosevelt went swimming there when the air temperature was twenty degrees below."

"It's a proven fact," said Patrick.

Lauren nodded. "There's a lifeguard on duty at the pool until nine-thirty at night every day of the year, except Christmas. And there's a walkway from the hotel over to the pool. And there's a giant slide into the big pool."

Patrick started to laugh. "Lauren, is there any research you haven't done?"

Lauren nodded. "I haven't read all the letters from famous people up in the hotel."

Patrick looked at his watch. "Okay, you girls can go over to the pool, but only for an hour or so. Then I want you to eat an early dinner and go to bed."

"I'm psyched to go to the pool, aren't you?" I said to Heidi.

Heidi looked distracted.

"You are coming, aren't you?"

Heidi bit her fingernail. She looked up at Patrick.

"What's wrong, Heidi?" Patrick asked.

"Before a big competition, shouldn't I go to my room and do visualization exercises?"

"Are you beginning to feel nervous?" Patrick asked Heidi.

She nodded. "Maybe I'm trying to come back too soon," Heidi said. "Maybe I've taken too much of a layoff. Maybe Mom was right."

"About what?" Patrick asked gently.

Heidi turned red. "Nothing," she said.

Patrick put his arm around Heidi. "Look, Heidi, I don't think sitting alone in your room is going to be good for you. Go with the Pinecones. Relax in the hot pool. I've been coaching you in the gym for a couple of months now. I *know* how strong you are."

"My body's strong," said Heidi, honestly. "It's my mind that worries me. Competition is in the mind."

"I have confidence your mind, your body, and your heart are ready for competition," said Patrick.

As I listened to Patrick, I relaxed for the first time in a long time. I had been so worked up about Madame Maria I had forgotten how much I liked Patrick.

Patrick saw me looking at him. He smiled at me. "Everybody's got nerves before a big competition, right, Cindi?"

"Come on, Heidi," I said. "You've been good for us. Without you, we would never have gotten good enough to come to the state championships. Let us teach you how to relax."

Heidi grinned. "It's a deal, guys. You teach me how to relax, and I'll teach you how to psych out the competition."

Heidi pointed across the lobby. The girls from Last Chance were dressed in swimsuits with sweatshirts over them and carrying towels.

Heidi shouted to them. "Hey, wait up," she shouted. "This is your Last Chance to go swimming with the Pinecones."

"Do Pinecones float?" asked Virginia turning her big glasses toward us.

"It's a proven fact," said Lauren.

"Virginia, meet the other Pinecones," said Heidi. "We're going to go to the hot springs, too."

"All of you?" asked Virginia.

Virginia looked at us as if she had just stepped in something unpleasant.

"What's her problem?" asked Darlene.

I shrugged.

"Maybe she just doesn't like to get so close to the competition," said Lauren.

12

Not My Idea
of Heaven

The pool temperature was delicious — that was the only word for it. I even got used to the smell. It was the biggest swimming pool I've ever seen. Two Olympic-size pools could have fit in the big pool, but the main thing was the temperature. In the small pool the water was almost too hot to stand, but in the big pool it was warm, just a little cooler than a bathtub. It was hard to describe. It felt as if it were a swimming pool on another planet.

The slide was nearly two stories high and was a twisting, covered tube. We bought tickets at the booth and wore our tickets on rubber bands around our wrists. Heidi was giggling as the Pinecones climbed the stairs.

"It's so high," she said.

"This from a girl who does a double back release from the high bar," I teased.

Lauren, Ti An, and Jodi went down the slide headfirst. Heidi looked a little anxious.

"Haven't you ever gone down a water slide before?" Darlene asked.

Heidi shook her head. "I never had time," she said. "If Mom saw me on top of this contraption, she'd have a conniption."

Darlene started laughing.

"What's so funny?" Heidi demanded.

"You and your family," said Darlene. "Your mom's not afraid to let you soar three feet above the high bar on a release move, but going down a water slide would scare her."

"I guess that is a little strange," admitted Heidi.

Virginia and the team from Last Chance were right behind us. Darlene went down the slide first.

"I can't believe your friend is a gymnast," said Virginia to Heidi and me.

"Darlene?" I asked.

Virginia nodded. I couldn't figure out why she'd be surprised that Darlene was a gymnast.

It wasn't exactly the height of the tourist season in Glenwood Springs. There were only about thirty people in the whole swimming pool, and I figured four out of five of them had to be gymnasts.

I started to go down the slide. "Oh, by the way," said Virginia, "why don't you come over to the little hot pool with us. I've got some quarters. You can use them to sit in these chairs that bubble."

"Neat," I said. "I'll tell my friends."

"Uh . . ." stammered Virginia, "I was thinking maybe just you. And of course, Heidi, if she wants."

"Super," said Heidi much quicker than I would have.

Darlene was standing shivering at the foot of the steps at the bottom of the slide. She yelled up to me. "What's the matter, Cindi and Heidi?" she shouted. "Are you chicken?"

"She sure has a loud voice," said Virginia. "But I guess she probably has to shout a lot in the ghetto."

I did a double take. Darlene in the ghetto was just about the funniest thing I could imagine.

"Go!" said Heidi.

I went down the slide on my stomach. Twisting and turning as I shot through the tube, I kept gathering speed. I didn't have time to think. It was exactly the same sensation I loved about gymnastics.

Lauren and Darlene were waiting. "Let's go in the real hot pool," said Lauren.

"Okay," I said. "Wait for Heidi. I think she wants to go, too. So do the girls from Last Chance."

Virginia came down the slide in front of Heidi. Her friend Helen was waiting for her, holding her glasses.

Virginia landed with a big splash, right on her butt. "I don't think she's going to be too much competition in the dance," giggled Jodi.

Virginia paddled to the side of the pool. She reached out for her glasses. Helen went to hand them to her, and slipped on the wet cement.

Darlene stuck her hand out to try to steady Helen, but Helen got startled by Darlene's touch. The glasses flew out of Helen's hand and started to fall into the pool. Lauren reached out for them and made an amazing catch, grabbing them by the earpiece. I clapped my hands together. "All right, Lauren. What a save!"

Lauren grinned. Virginia pulled herself out of the pool and grabbed her eyeglasses from Lauren. When she did, she pulled the earpiece off.

"Look what you did!" Virginia yelled.

68

Lauren shook her head in confusion. "Sorry," she said quickly, although I didn't think she had anything to be sorry about. Darlene and Lauren had just been trying to save Virginia's glasses.

"It wasn't her fault," said Darlene.

Heidi came splashing down from the top of the slide. She had a big grin on her face, like a little kid. "Wow!" she exclaimed. "That was terrific!" Heidi pulled herself out of the pool. "Let's go to the hot pool. I can't believe I'm having this much fun the day before a meet."

Virginia kept fiddling with her broken glasses. "You can put them together with a safety pin," Darlene said. "They're not really broken."

"They're the only pair I've got for the competition," said Virginia. "I'll look great in front of the judges." She glared at Darlene. "I think you did it on purpose! You're just nasty. All you people are nasty."

"We are not!" I protested.

"I wasn't talking about you," said Virginia. She glared at Darlene.

"I think she meant people of my color," said Darlene softly.

"I *didn't* say that," protested Virginia.

"No, but that's what you meant, isn't it?" asked Darlene.

Heidi looked from one to the other. "This is

silly," she said. "We're all gymnasts. Let's just go to the hot pool."

"That's where I'm going," said Virginia as she and the other girls from Last Chance stalked off.

Heidi grabbed my arm. "Come on," she said. "Let's go sit in those chairs they were talking about."

"I'm not going where I'm not wanted," said Darlene.

"I'm cold," said Jodi. "I'm ready to go back to the hotel."

"Me, too," said Ti An. She was shivering. So was Ashley.

"I'm ready to go back," said Lauren. They gathered up their towels and left. Darlene started to pack up, too.

Heidi shook her head. "Look, I don't know what happened, but I'll let you in on a secret about competition. It pays to be charming to the opposition. You lure them into liking you, and then you zap them."

I looked at Heidi. "That doesn't make much sense."

"Sure it does," she said. "Come on." Heidi didn't hesitate. She rushed off to the hot pool.

"Uh . . ." I hesitated.

"You can go," said Darlene. "You're the right color."

70

"Darlene," I protested. "I was the one who wanted to stand up for you to Madame Maria."

"Madame Maria doesn't hold a candle to those turkeys," said Darlene. "I can smell the difference. It's stronger than the sulphur in the pool."

"Why don't we just go to the hot pool together?" I begged.

"They don't want me," said Darlene. "They only want you."

"Well, I won't go," I said.

Darlene sighed. "Go on. Maybe you can out-psych the competition. Besides, I'm tired. I'm going back to my hotel room with the others."

"Heidi said we should out-psych them," I argued. "You come, too. Virginia even said that wasn't what she meant."

"Those weren't exactly her words," said Darlene. "Why don't you just listen to your new friends for a while?"

"They're not really my new friends," I protested. "It seems silly to come all this way and just stick with people we know."

"Right," said Darlene, giving me a very strange look. "Stick with your own kind."

"Darlene," I said. "That's not fair."

She shook her head. "No," she said. "It isn't." Darlene started to gather up her things.

Heidi came running up. She was grinning.

"Come on," she said. "The hot pool is so neat! In those chairs the bubbles come right up. It's heaven."

"It's not my idea of heaven," said Darlene, wrapping the towel around her.

"What's wrong with her?" Heidi asked.

I watched Darlene go. "Darlene thinks Virginia's prejudiced against her because she's black."

"Oh, don't be silly," said Heidi. "Darlene's just being oversensitive. Come on."

And I went.

13

Roll with the Punches

The bubbles surrounded me. I floated on top of a metal chair with holes in it. A quarter gave you five minutes of bubbles. It was impossible not to giggle. Heidi looked at me with a big grin on her face.

"Now, *this* is how to relax before a competition," she said. "I might have to buy one of these chairs and take it with me. I can put it in the bathtub when I go to Indianapolis for the worlds."

"This is so cool," said Virginia. "To sit in the hot pool with Heidi Ferguson and her friend."

"Not all of her friends," I said. I still felt uneasy about the fact that the other Pinecones weren't there.

Virginia stretched her legs out so she floated above the bubbles. She had big black-and-blue marks on her upper thighs, probably from hitting the lower bar hard in her uneven bars routine. We gymnasts are always black and blue.

She looked tough. Her legs looked incredibly strong. "I don't think your 'other' friend would be comfortable in the pool with us," said Virginia.

"Excuse me?" I asked. "What does that mean?"

Helen floated over from her chair and whispered something in Virginia's ear. Virginia shooed her away as if she were a pesky fly.

"Helen's worried that I'm going to make you mad, if I tell you what I really think."

"I think this conversation is getting far too serious for relaxing in hot water," Heidi said.

"Come on, Virginia," I challenged. "I want to know what you really think."

"Cindi," warned Heidi, "maybe you should take a dip in the cooler pool."

"It's nothing personal," said Virginia. "For example, even though you're from the city, I think you're all right."

"You don't know anything about me," I said.

Heidi looked over at me. She saw how mad I was getting. "Cindi, don't get worked up over nothing."

Virginia stretched her legs out again. "I just think that people should stick to their own kind. My mom and dad think the same way I do. They taught me that animals stick to their own kind. People should do the same. Don't you agree, Heidi?"

"I don't get involved with politics," said Heidi.

"This isn't politics," I said.

Heidi floated over to me. "Cindi," she hissed, "don't pick a fight with them. *That's* bad politics."

"What are you two whispering about?" Virginia asked.

"We were just talking over strategy for tomorrow's competition," said Heidi.

"We're going to win," said Virginia smugly. I wanted to wipe that smug grin off her face, but I was afraid to pick a real fight. Heidi knew a lot more about serious competition than I did. Maybe she was right that we should try to trick the Last Chance team into liking us.

I got out of the pool. "What's wrong?" Heidi asked.

I grabbed my towel. "I'm going back to the hotel," I said through gritted teeth. Heidi looked at the clock. "I guess I'd better be going, too," she said.

"Hey, girls," said Virginia, turning in the pool.

"Tomorrow night our coach is throwing a party, and you are invited."

"What about the rest of the team?" I asked Virginia.

"I don't think they'd be comfortable there," said she. "Most of the other kids will be from small towns."

"Then why do you think Heidi and I would fit in?" I asked.

Virginia just smiled at me.

Before I could tell Virginia what she could do with her invitation, Heidi answered for me. "Thanks for the invite," she said. "I'm sure we'll want to stop in."

"I'm not," I hissed.

"Shh," warned Heidi as we started back to the hotel room. "Don't make waves before the competition. Besides, the party might be fun."

"We can't go to a party that the other Pinecones aren't invited to," I said.

"Why not?" asked Heidi. "The Pinecones aren't joined at the hip, are they? Maybe we'll go to the party, maybe we won't, but you don't have to pick a big fight about it now. It's the wrong time. You don't need negative vibes before a big meet."

I looked back at the girls from Last Chance. "They're a bunch of racists," I said.

"Cindi, Cindi," said Heidi, as if she were ten years, not just a few years, older than me. "You

76

meet all kinds at competitions. You've got to roll with the punches."

"You certainly have learned how to do that," I said. I didn't like the way I was acting, either. I had a feeling that some punches you shouldn't roll with.

14

Sportswomanship

I didn't sleep well. I kept telling myself that it was just because I was nervous about the competition. I tried to get rid of negative vibes. I kept repeating what Heidi had said to me — no negative vibes before a big meet.

But the negative vibes weren't just in my head. Darlene and I had hardly talked when I came back from the pool. She had been polite, but real distant, as if we were roommates by chance and not friends. Dinner had been stilted and awkward, not just between Darlene and me, but between all of us.

I think I had finally fallen asleep for about fifteen minutes when there was a knock on the door. "Girls," said Patrick, softly. "It's six A.M. Time to get up."

Darlene pulled the covers up over her head.

"It's totally unfair," she complained. "Why do we have to compete at eighty-thirty in the morning? Why are we first?"

"Because we're not the elites," I said. "Heidi's the one who'll be in prime time. At least we'll all have the same disadvantages. Think about it, maybe those girls from Last Chance hate the mornings as much as you do."

"Fat chance," mumbled Darlene. "I'm sure they've all been raised on the farm and just *love* getting up with the sun. I bet they think that *my* people laze around all day."

"Darlene," I protested, "come on, you work harder and are smarter than anybody I know. Don't talk like that."

"Did you tell your friends in the hot pool that?" asked Darlene.

"They're just silly girls," I said. "Heidi said that I shouldn't rile them up."

"Oh, right," said Darlene. "Heidi really knows everything, doesn't she?"

"Well, she's been at a lot more competitions than we have," I said.

"Yeah," said Darlene. She gave me a funny look as she went into the bathroom. I sat down on my bed. I felt rotten.

Patrick was just about the only cheery one when we went downstairs to breakfast. Lauren wouldn't look at me, and she only picked at her toast.

"Lauren, is something wrong?" asked Patrick. "I don't blame you for being nervous before a competition, but it's not like you not to eat anything."

"It's nothing," said Lauren. She looked up. Just then the Last Chance team filed into the dining room. Darlene had been right. They all looked as bright-eyed and bushy-tailed as characters from Disney World. They already had on their leotards, and they wore matching ribbons in their hair.

"Uh-oh," said Lauren. "Here comes the enemy."

"The Last Chance team," said Patrick. "I know their coach. She's tough. They've won your division every year for the past five years. But you can take them."

"I don't *want* them," said Darlene. Just then a peculiar perfume wafted through the dining room. Madame Maria swept in, dressed all in black except for a blue-and-rose scarf she was wearing around her head with the ends trailing practically to her rear end.

The Last Chance team stared at her as if she were the most exotic thing ever to cross the border into Colorado. They giggled when she sat down at our table.

"This is the most uncivilized hour I've ever heard of to force dancers to perform."

"We're not dancers, Madame Maria. We're gymnasts," I said.

"It doesn't matter," said Madame Maria. "The principle is the same. Even in the Soviet Union when we took classes all day, we would never be asked to get up at this hour. Bodies cannot warm up at this hour."

"Madame Maria," said Darlene, "I think you're absolutely right. Maybe you can protest to the judges for us."

Madame Maria smiled at Darlene. "They probably wouldn't listen to me," she said. "Instead, I will just have to be sure that I rrrroot for you." Madame Maria exaggeratedly trilled the word *root*. She smiled. It had never occurred to me that Madame Maria could make fun of her own accent.

Madame Maria looked around the table at us. "Girls, I know I was hard on some of you while you were training with me. Especially you, Darlene, I pushed you hard. You had talent and confidence in dance, that, for example, Cindi and Jodi didn't. I only wanted you to do better. Now I know that you are nervous, but that is good. You will use those nerves only to do better."

Patrick nodded his head in agreement.

Heidi bounded into the dining room. She gave a big friendly wave to the girls from the Last Chance team, and then she came over to our table.

"What are you doing up so early?" Patrick asked. "I told you you could sleep late if you wanted."

"I need to cheer on the Pinecones," said Heidi. "Besides, I can never sleep before a big competition."

"I couldn't, either," I confessed.

After that there was dead silence around the table. Even with Madame Maria's pep talk, it was as if a cloud were over us, and I didn't think it was just nerves.

"All right, girls," said Patrick. "It's time to be getting to the gym. I know your nerves are all tingling, but you don't have to be quite so glum. We're here to have fun as well as to compete."

Heidi shook her head. "Patrick, that's fine to *say*, but you don't really believe it, do you?"

Patrick nodded his head. "Absolutely," he said. "It should never stop being fun."

"I don't agree," said Heidi. "There comes a moment when sports are like war."

"Heidi," warned Patrick, "that's the attitude that's gotten you in trouble in the past."

82

"It's the attitude that got me to the world championships," said Heidi defiantly.

"And then . . ." said Patrick.

Heidi blushed.

"It's a sport, Heidi. It's not war. It's not even war games. You've got to remember that."

"I don't think the team from Last Chance believes that," said Jodi.

"Then you girls will have to teach them a lesson in sportsmanship."

"Sportswomanship," I corrected Patrick.

"You're right, Cindi," he said. I had a feeling that I hadn't been right about much lately. I had been wrong about Madame Maria. She had explained why she had been hard on Darlene, and her explanation made sense. But the girls from Last Chance hadn't had to make explanations. I had just let their comments about "our kind" and "people like her from the ghetto" go. The girls from Last Chance had judged Darlene without knowing anything about her. And the worse thing was they thought I agreed with them. They thought I wanted to stick with my "own kind," too.

"Okay, girls," said Patrick. "Let's get into the van and over to the gym. And Pinecones, do me a favor?"

"What's that?" asked Jodi.

"Lighten up," said Patrick. "Lighten up."

"That's exactly what the team from Last Chance would like," muttered Darlene. "They'd like me to 'lighten up.' "

Patrick looked confused by her comments, but I knew exactly what Darlene meant.

15

Not Champions
in My Book

I expected something a little more spectacular for the state championships. The gym was nice enough. It was a new high school gym, very light and airy with light coming in through skylights at either end of the basketball court. The entire floor was covered with blue mats, and the areas for the different apparatus were roped off. The judges from the USGF were already bustling around with their clipboards in hands. Just seeing those clipboards made me nervous.

But the bleachers were practically empty. There was a snack bar at one end selling doughnuts, orange juice, and coffee. There was another little stand selling banners and leotards and gymnastics pins.

Patrick signed us in with the officials. He told us to go over to the sidelines and put down our gym bags. The team from Last Chance had already begun to warm up.

Darlene deliberately went to the farthest end away from me. Lauren went with her. Patrick watched us. I put my gym bag down and started to take out my gym shoes.

"Cindi," said Patrick. "What's going on with the Pinecones?" he asked.

"Nothing," I said.

"Ever since you kids went to the pool late yesterday, you've been acting strange," he said. "It's not just nerves. I can tell."

"Patrick," I asked. "Have you ever met anybody who didn't like black people? Or, I guess, anybody who's different from them?"

Patrick frowned. "Cindi, I know Madame Maria has strange ways. She may be old-fashioned, and maybe she's wrong about a few things, but she's good-hearted. She really does want to help the team. She came here at her own expense."

"I'm not talking about Madame Maria," I said.

I told Patrick about the little digs that the team from Last Chance made. "Virginia says that animals stick to their own kind and people should, too."

"That sounds racist to me," said Patrick.

I think I was hoping Patrick would tell me I

was all wrong. "Heidi told me not to make waves. What should I have done? Should I have told them off?"

Patrick looked across the bleachers. "Heidi," he said, "come down here a moment, will you?"

Heidi came down. "Want me to give the Pinecones a last-minute pep talk?" she asked.

"No," said Patrick. "I want to know if what Cindi tells me about the team from Last Chance is true."

Heidi shrugged. "It's got nothing to do with gymnastics," she said. "They just don't like kids from the city."

"They like you and me just fine," I objected. "They don't *know* us. 'Kids from the city' are just code words for anybody who's not white."

Darlene and Lauren came over to us. "What's going on?" Darlene asked. "Shouldn't we be warming up?"

"I told Patrick about the team from Last Chance," I said to Darlene. "I told him I think they're racists."

I looked at Patrick. "What *do* you think I should I have done?" I asked.

Heidi interrupted before Patrick could answer. "It's a terrible idea to make things personal," she said. "You don't want to give them a reason to want to beat you. Just let it go."

"I wanted to tell them that they're stupid," I

said. "I wanted to tell them that *all* of us Pine-cones are good friends, and that I think their beliefs are stupid."

"You can't tell them that," hissed Heidi. "It's better to keep your mouth shut and then whip their butts in competition."

"That might not be the Pinecone way," said Patrick. "I'm not even sure it's the best way. What's stopping you, Cindi?"

"Darlene, do you really think I should confront them?" I said.

"Maybe I should have done it myself," she said.

"You kids are crazy," said Heidi. "You shouldn't be messing with something like this right before a meet. It's got nothing to do with gymnastics."

"It's got everything to do with who the Pine-cones are, Heidi," said Patrick.

"Why don't you go tell them off, Patrick?" I begged.

Patrick shook his head. "On that issue, Heidi's right. This isn't about gymnastics, and I wasn't there. It's up to you."

I looked at Darlene. "Come on, Darlene. We've got something to take care of."

"But . . . but . . ." stammered Heidi, "you're going to make the team from Last Chance mad. They're going to go out of their way to try to beat you."

"Heidi," I said, "we're the Pinecones. We're not scared of them."

"They're champions," said Heidi. "You don't want to give a champion a reason to hate you."

"They're not champions in my book," I said. "I want them to know it."

16

We'll Wipe the Floor with You

"What are you going to say to them?" Darlene asked me.

"I'm not sure," I admitted. "All I know is that I felt rotten all night because I had kept my mouth shut."

The team from Last Chance was already warming up on the beam. I went over and politely waited while Virginia finished her routine. I was pleased, though, that her glasses did look kind of funny with a safety pin sticking out of them. Unfortunately she was a really good gymnast.

She saw Darlene and me standing on the edge

of the mats when she did her dismount. "What do you want?" she asked. "The Pinecones are supposed to warm up on the vault now."

"I wanted to talk to you about the way you've been acting, particularly toward my friend Darlene," I said.

"Is that your name?" asked Virginia to Darlene.

"Yes," I said. "Isn't it funny that you learned my name and Heidi's name, but you couldn't learn Darlene's?"

"Do you have a point?" asked Virginia.

"Yes," I said. "You'd better learn that you can't tell what *kind* of person someone is by the color of her skin. Darlene's one of my best friends. And we do stick to our own kind. We're the nice kind."

"Oh, give me a break," said Virginia. "And what kind does that make me?"

"The nasty kind," I said. "The kind that's too stupid to look around and find out what's right."

"Just one minute," said Virginia. "You know, you city kids think you're so sharp."

"We're not so sharp," I said. "We just don't prejudge who we're going to be friends with."

"You didn't talk that way yesterday in the pool," said Virginia.

"That's because I was stupid yesterday," I said. "Today I'm not."

"I think you are," said Virginia. "And, by the way . . . our team is going to wipe the floor with you."

"No, you're not," said Darlene.

"Now it's personal," said Virginia. "We're going to show you city kids that it doesn't pay to mess with us."

"We'll see," I said.

The other Pinecones were waiting with Patrick, Madame Maria, and Heidi when we came back. "What happened?" asked Heidi anxiously.

"Cindi was terrific," said Darlene. "She told them they were nasty. She said that the Pinecones don't judge anybody by the color of their skin."

Madame Maria nodded her head. "Very good, Cindi," she trilled.

"What did they say?" asked Lauren.

"They said they were going to wipe the floor with us," I admitted.

"We'll show them," said Jodi.

"Girls, whatever happens, I'm proud of you," said Patrick.

"Come off it, Patrick," I said. "Admit it, don't you want us to wipe them out?"

"Well," drawled Patrick. "I wouldn't mind. Now let's get started. Cindi's right. It would be very,

very nice to tell the team from Last Chance that they've had their last chance."

"Do you really think the Pinecones can do it?" asked Heidi.

"Of course I do," said Patrick. "Now, let's go for it! It's personal now."

 *17*

Wait Till
Next Year

The judges were incredible sticklers. They deducted penalties for things that we had never lost points for before. We fell behind on the uneven bars when Lauren lost five-tenths of a point just on her first mount. We kept being whittled to death by tiny deductions.

Ti An did a beautiful beam routine, but she went on past the bell for her landing, and right away that lost us another event.

The team from Last Chance didn't make any major mistakes. It wasn't that they were *that* much better than we were. It's just that they never muffed a move.

"I warned you," said Heidi, who looked more miserable over the fact that we were losing than we did. "I told you not to give the other team an edge. You've got them fired up."

"Heidi," said Patrick impatiently. "Look at the scores."

"I have," said Heidi. "It's hopeless. The Pinecones have fallen so far behind there's nothing they can do to make up the difference. There's only the dance competition left. The team from Last Chance can't lose. No matter what the team from Last Chance does, they've already won."

"I mean *look* at the scores," said Patrick. "Who has a chance to sew up second place?"

"The Pinecones," admitted Heidi. "They're ahead of the team from Grand Junction, but just barely. And the Atomic Amazons are right behind Grand Junction."

"Great," I muttered. "We can prove to Last Chance that we're second best."

"No!" said Patrick sharply. "You've already proved to them that you're not."

"Here it comes," said Darlene, sounding depressed. "The moral victory speech."

"Yes," said Patrick. "And it's not just a moral victory. Nobody expected me to bring a team to the state championships. You Pinecones have pulled yourselves together. The team from Last Chance has been coming to the state championships for a dozen years. They expect to win. Heidi's right, you can't catch up. Even if you girls pull off a spectacular dance competition, you won't win the tournament, but you sure can give the team from Last Chance something to worry about next year."

"You know, Patrick," said Heidi, "I like the way you think. If they can win the dance requirement, the team from Last Chance will remember that the next time they meet the Pinecones. It's always harder to stay on top than it is to get there. The team from Last Chance won't feel that much like celebrating tonight."

"We still have to *win* the dance in order to come in second," I reminded Heidi. "We don't have an absolute lock on dance. It's not a sure thing."

"But you've got a good shot," said Patrick. "Now, girls, remember everything that Madame Maria taught you."

Madame Maria gathered her skirts around her and thrust herself into the middle of our huddle. "Each of you, just imagine that there is a light shining from inside your chest. You *must* make everyone want to look at you. And feel the music. The music must be part of you. You all know the routine by heart. You are dancers, each of you. It *must* flow. You must float like beautiful butterflies over the mats."

"Butterflies with airy armpits," I said.

Madame Maria frowned. Then she smiled.

"Whatever works," she said in her thick accent. "And most of all . . ."

"Yes?" Darlene asked. She was hanging on every word Madame Maria was saying.

"Most of all . . ." repeated Madame Maria, "kick butt."

I cracked up.

"But beautifully," added Madame Maria. "Do it like the dancer that each of you is."

"Thank you, Madame Maria," said Patrick. "I couldn't have said it better myself."

The judges called to us to finish our warm-ups. I stood to the side. The dance routine is mercifully short. It lasts only ninety seconds. The team from Last Chance went first. As usual they did every element of the dance routine without making any mistakes.

Then it was our turn. Ti An performed flawlessly, but the judges didn't think so. They deducted points for insufficient height on her leaps, even though to me it looked like Ti An was flying.

Still, she got a high enough score to keep us in the running, and so did Lauren and Ashley. They both performed better than I had ever seen them. But the judges didn't give them great scores.

"It's up to you and Darlene," said Patrick. "You

can still pull us away from Grand Junction. Just remember what Madame Maria said."

"The 'float like the butterfly' part or the 'kick butt' part?" asked Darlene.

"Both," said Patrick.

I stood next to Patrick as Darlene walked onto the mats. She held her rib cage high. She looked beautiful. The girls from Last Chance were giggling and poking each other, obviously doing anything to distract her. I gave them dirty looks, but they didn't stop.

Darlene didn't look at them. The music started. Even the girls from Last Chance had to stop giggling. It was impossible not to watch Darlene. She didn't look like she was performing a compulsory routine. She looked like she was inspired by the music.

Patrick bit his lip as Darlene finished. She ran off the mats. Patrick gave her a hug. "That was beautiful," he said.

The judges gave Darlene a perfect 10.

Darlene couldn't believe it. She squealed and jumped up and down. Madame Maria opened up her arms and hugged Darlene, too. "Today, you were a dancer," she said.

I took a deep breath.

"Okay, Cindi," said Patrick. "You can do it. It's up to you."

I closed my eyes. If only it were a vault or an

uneven bar routine — anything but dance.

I felt somebody hug me. I opened my eyes. It was Darlene. "I'll never do it," I said.

"Come on, Cindi," teased Darlene. "You're not just doing it for the Pinecones — you've got to prove that white kids really can dance."

"Darlene!" I started laughing, and the laughter relaxed me.

Darlene giggled. I heard the judges call my name. I took a deep breath and walked out onto the mats.

Virginia sneered at me. Her team knew they had the competition already sewed up. I glared back at her. I crossed my arms in front of my chest. I thought I actually saw Virginia stick her tongue out at me. Maybe I imagined it, but I don't think so. Darlene had her hands on her hips, staring right back at Virginia.

Then I heard the music. I opened my arms. Suddenly I was breathing with the music. It felt as if I had all the time in the world. The music was the walls, and I stretched with the beat, touching all the corners. My upper body seemed to have helium balloons pulling me up, so that everything was less work than ever before. All the endless practice had been just for this moment.

Then it was as if I were coming out of a trance. I saw Patrick raise his fist in the air.

I saluted the judges and trotted off the mats. "Beautiful, Cindi," he said, but I could tell that he was nervous about my score.

I looked back at the judges' stand. My score came up. 9.63. I couldn't believe it. I had actually scored my highest score ever on dance. We had second place locked up. The Pinecones were hugging and cheering.

The girls from Last Chance stared at us. Virginia and Helen walked by. "I can't believe you girls are so excited about winning second place," said Virginia. "I told you we'd wipe the floor with you, and we did."

Virginia stalked away. Helen started to follow her. Darlene still had her hands on her hips. Helen struck out her hand.

"Congratulations," she said to Darlene. "That's the first ten I've seen them give to a level six."

Darlene hesitated and then shook Helen's hand. "Thanks," she said.

Helen seemed embarrassed. "Uh . . . you know, Virginia sometimes says things . . . she doesn't mean anything by them."

"Yeah, right," I said. I didn't believe Helen. I thought Virginia knew exactly what she was saying.

Virginia came up and practically grabbed

Helen. "Come on," she said impatiently. "We've got to get ready for the awards. Remember, we're the team that won!"

"Wait till next year," I warned her. "Just wait till next year."

About the Author

Elizabeth Levy decided that the only way she could write about gymnastics was to try it herself. Besides taking classes, she is involved with a group of young gymnasts near her home in New York City, and enjoys following their progress.

Elizabeth Levy's other Apple Paperbacks are *A Different Twist, The Computer That Said Steal Me,* and all the other books in THE GYMNASTS series.

She likes visiting schools to give talks and meet her readers. Kids love her presentations. Why? "I sometimes end with a cartwheel!" says Levy. "At least I try to."

WIN A TRIP TO THE 1991 WORLD GYMNASTICS CHAMPIONSHIPS

We'll send the Winner of this random drawing and his/her parent or guardian (age 21 or older) to the exciting 1991 WORLD GYMNASTICS CHAMPIONSHIPS in Indianapolis, Indiana! The trip includes:

★ Hotel — 3 nights! (September 13, 14 and 15, 1991)
★ Round-trip airline tickets!
★ 2 premium seat tickets to major championship events!

Just fill in the coupon below and return it by May 31, 1991.

Rules: Entries must be postmarked by May 31, 1991. Winner will be picked at random and notified by mail. Parent or guardian must be age 21 or older. No purchase necessary. Valid only in the U.S. Void where prohibited. Taxes on prizes are the responsibility of the winner and his/hers immediate family. Employees of Scholastic Inc.; its agencies, affiliates, subsidiaries; and their immediate families not eligible.

Fill in the coupon or write the information on a 3" x 5" piece of paper and mail to: 1991 WORLD GYMNASTICS CHAMPIONSHIPS, Scholastic Inc., P.O. Box 755, New York, NY 10003.

1991 World Gymnastics Championships

Name _____ Age _____

Street _____

City _____ State _____ Zip _____

Where did you buy this *Gymnasts* book?

❑ Bookstore   ❑ Drugstore   ❑ Supermarket   ❑ Library

❑ Book Club   ❑ Book Fair   ❑ Other _____ (specify)

GYM790

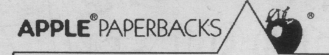

APPLE® PAPERBACKS

by Elizabeth Levy

SLEEPOVER FRIENDS™

by Susan Saunders

Available wherever you buy books...or use this order form.